What Goes Up?

by Tess Samson

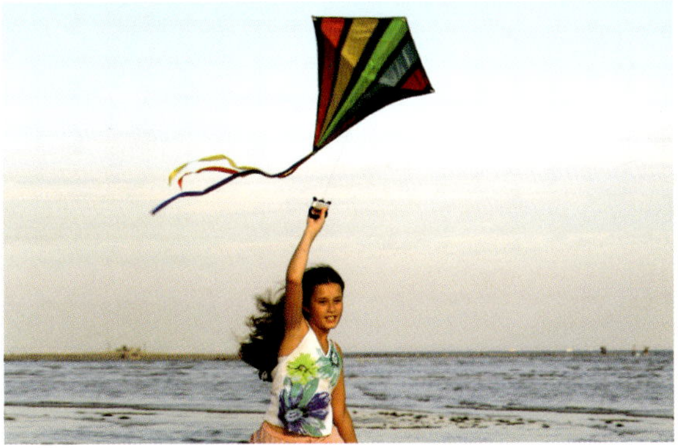
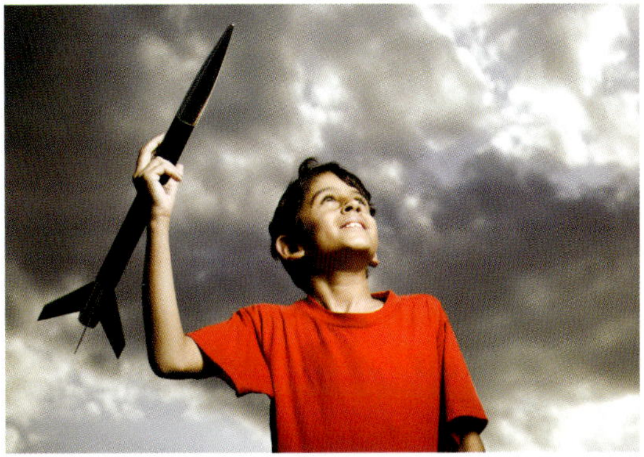
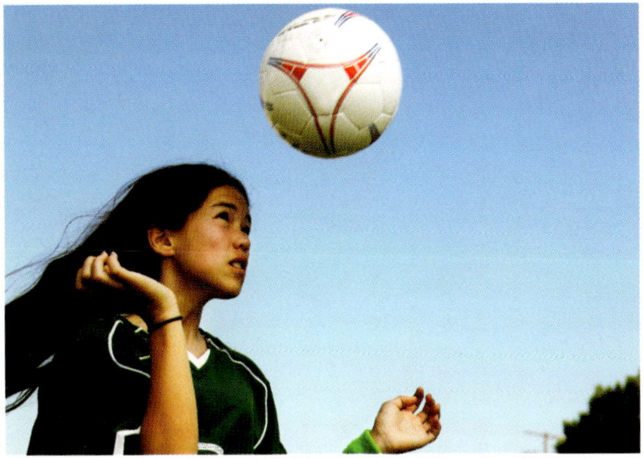
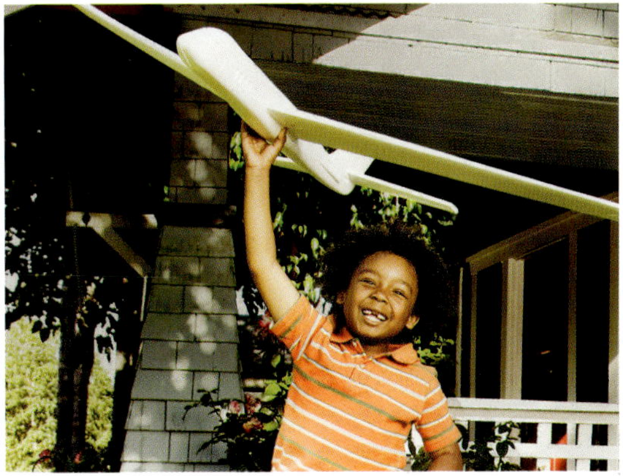

Picture Words

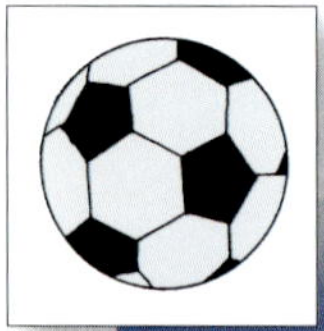

ball

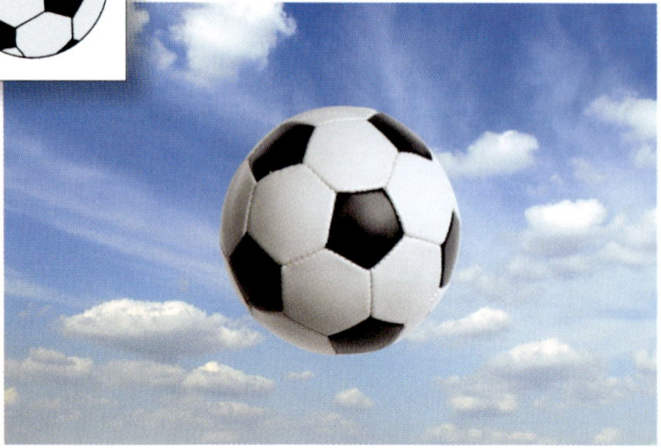

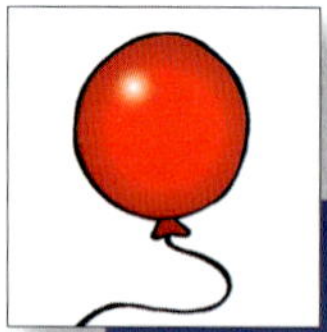

balloon

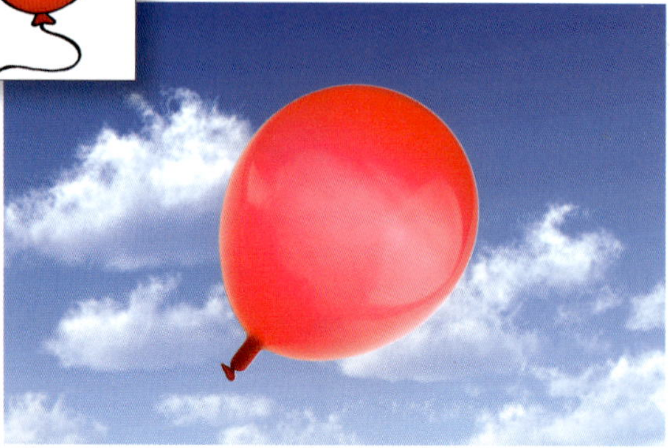

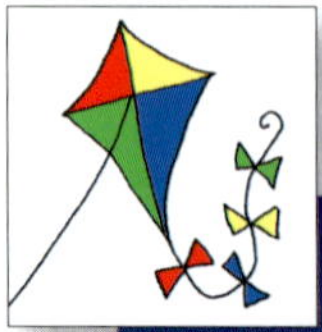

kite

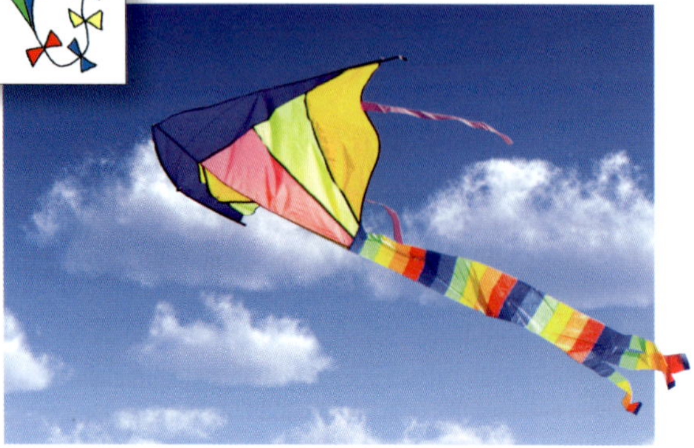

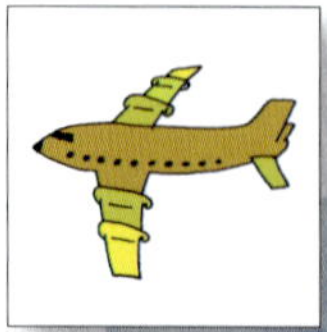

plane

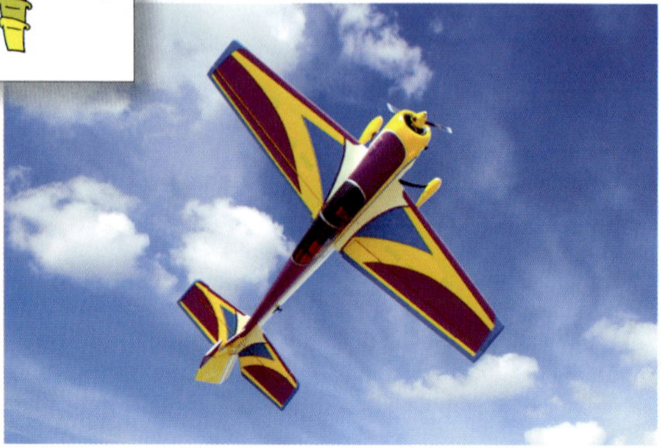

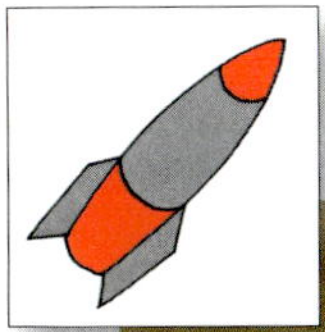

rocket

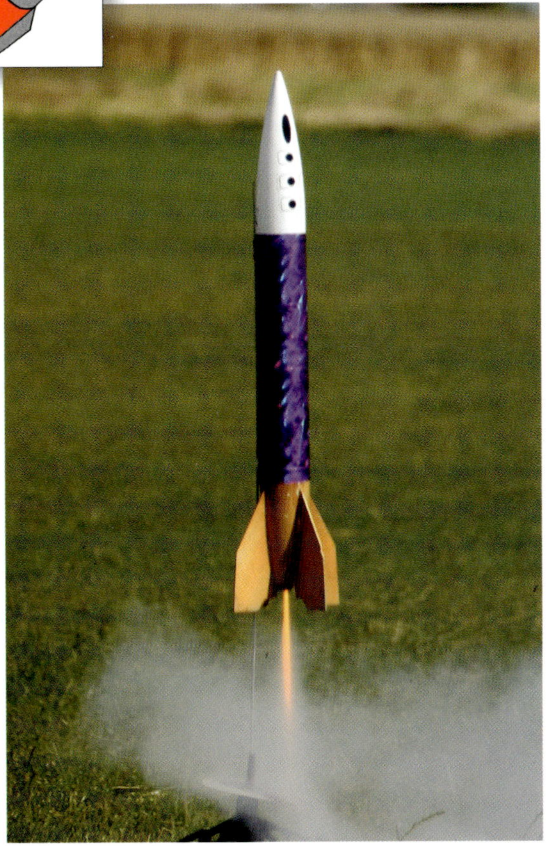

Sight Words

goes

that

up

That 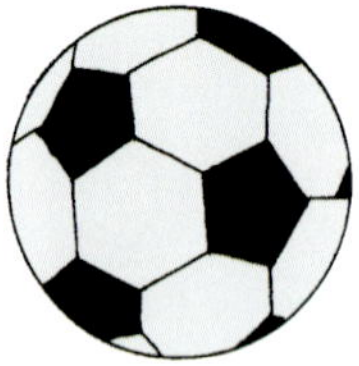 goes up.

ball

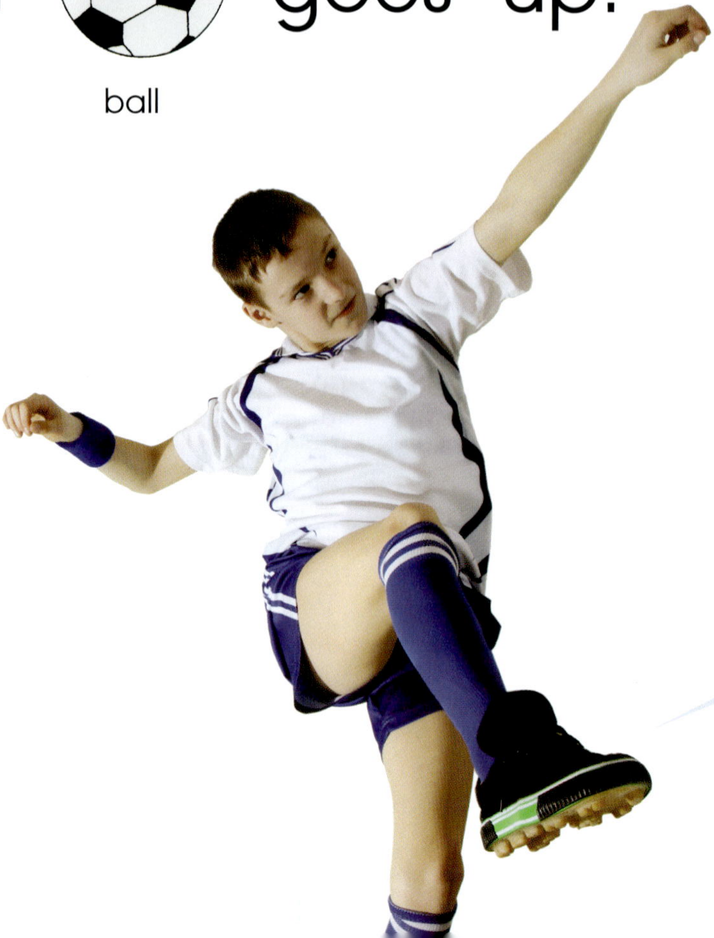

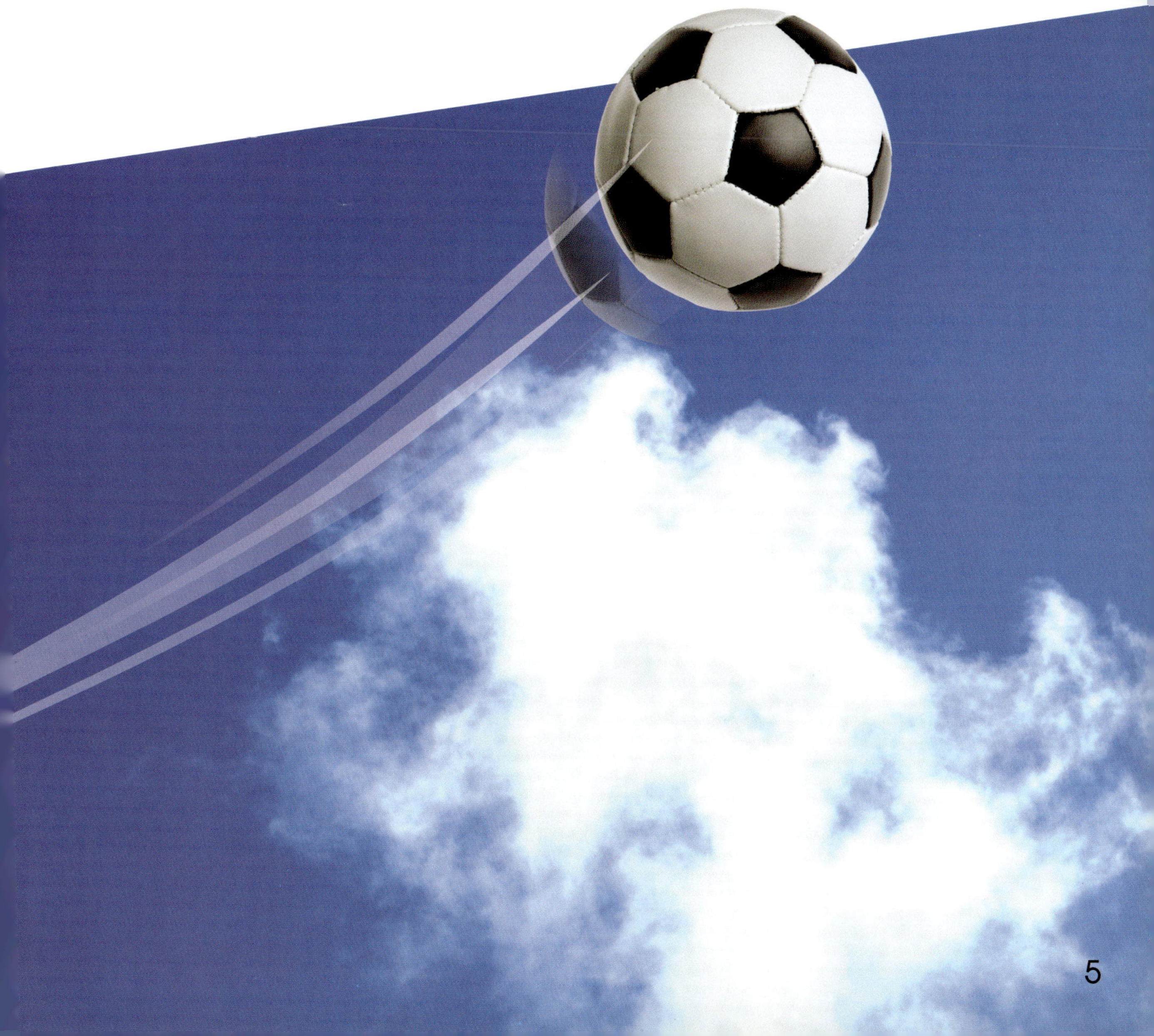

That 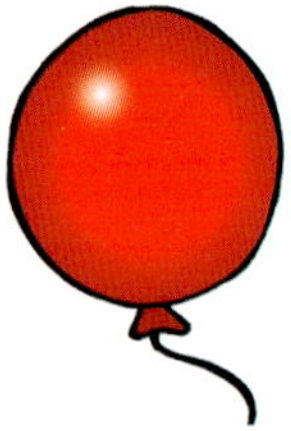 goes up.

balloon

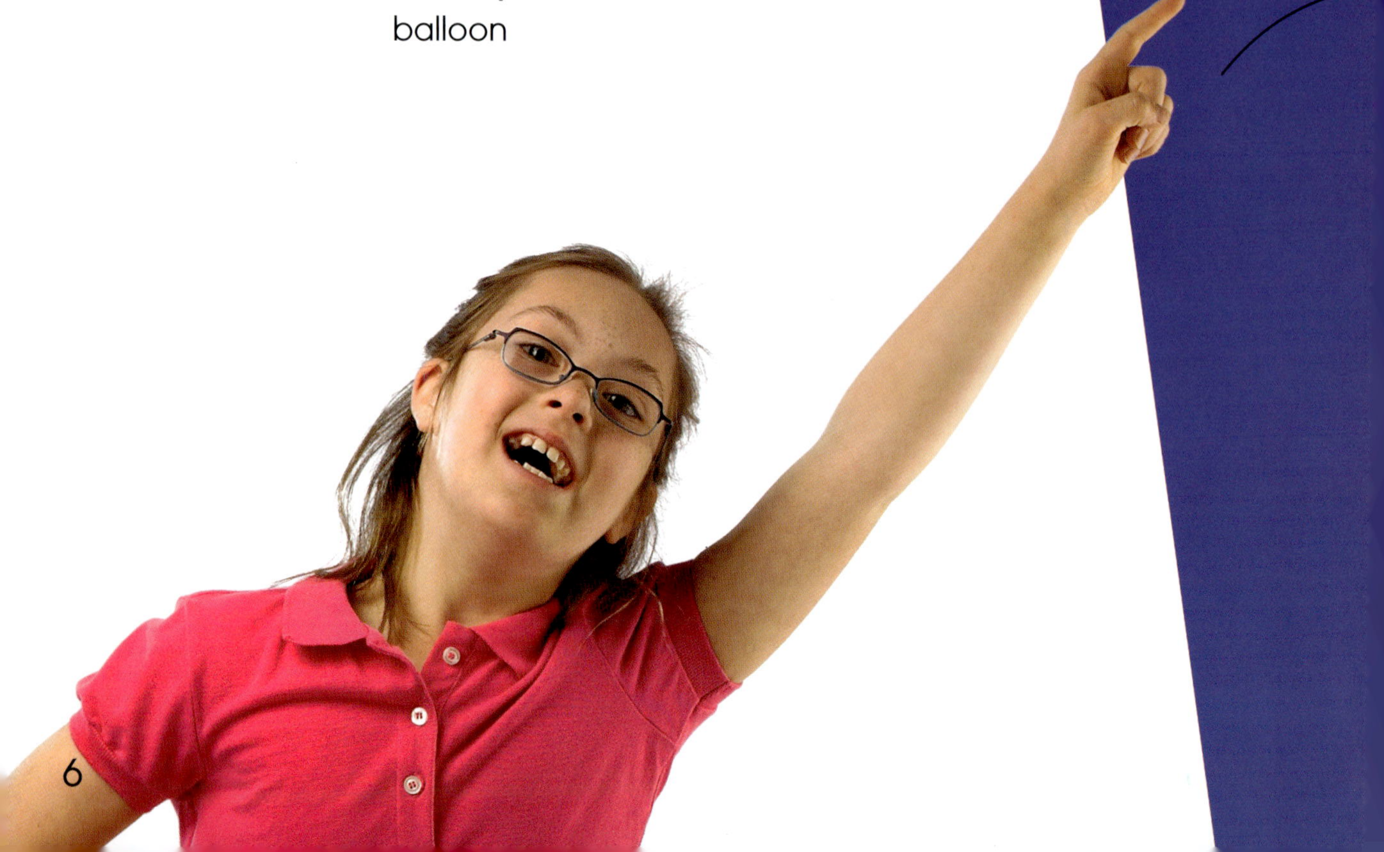

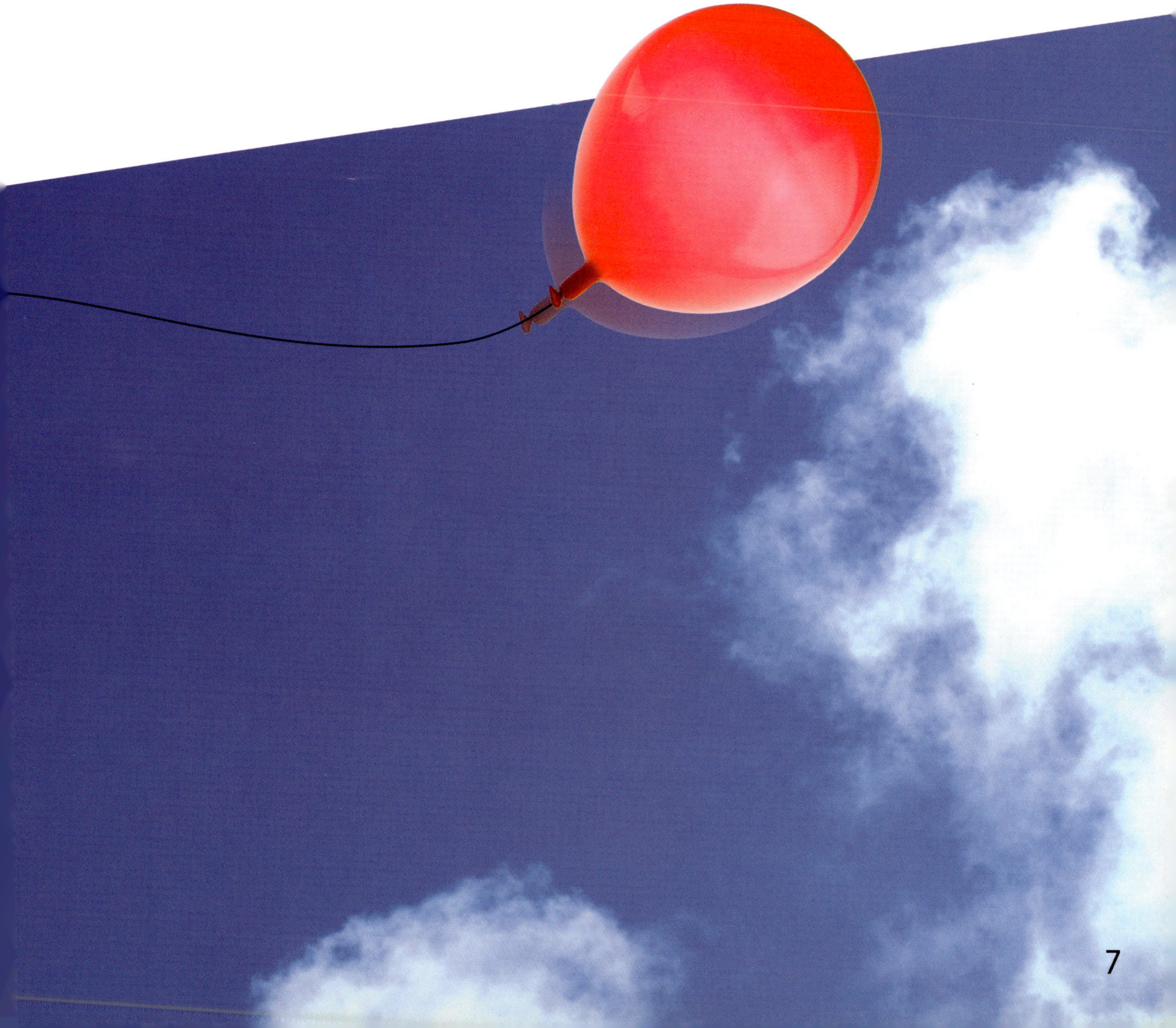

That 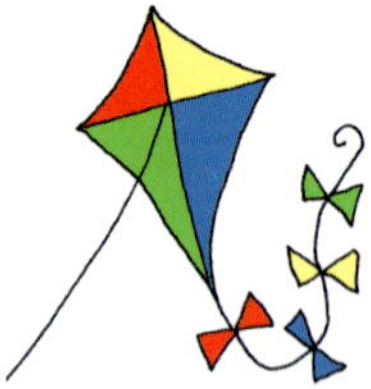 goes up.

kite

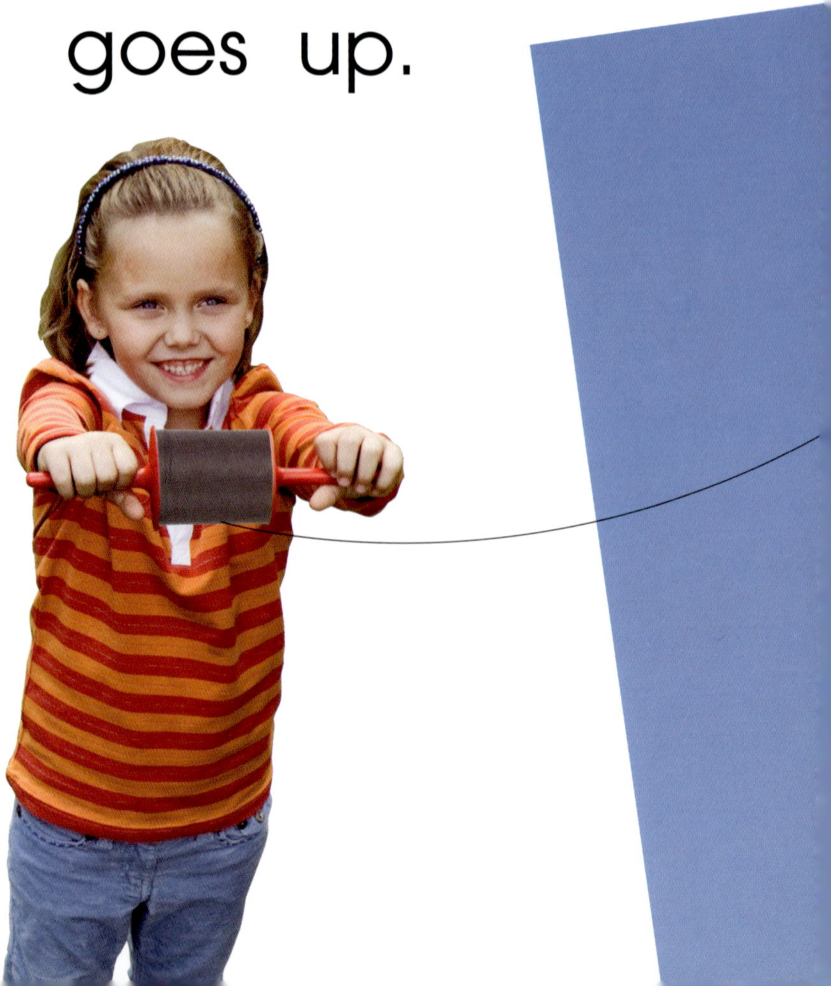

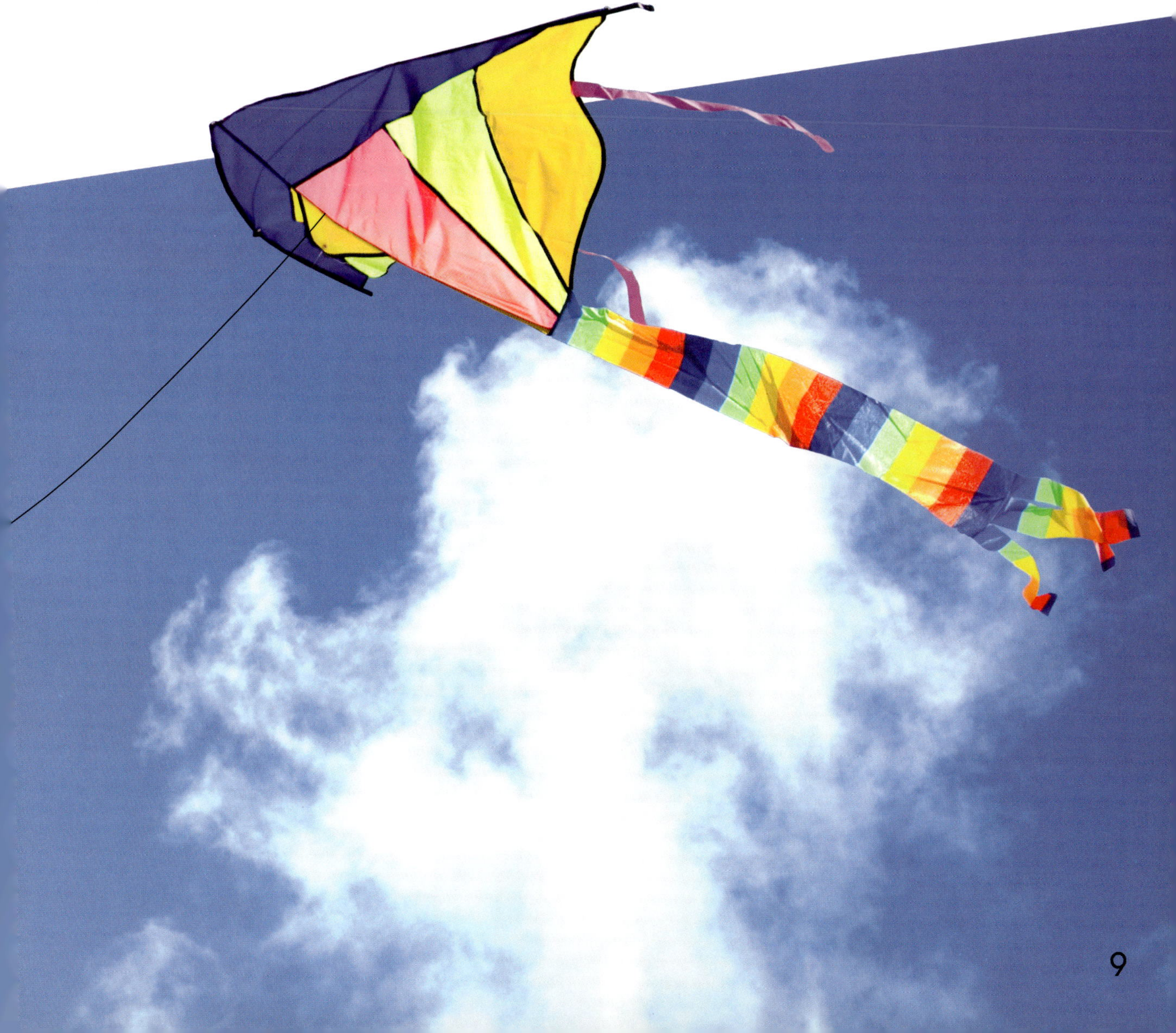

That 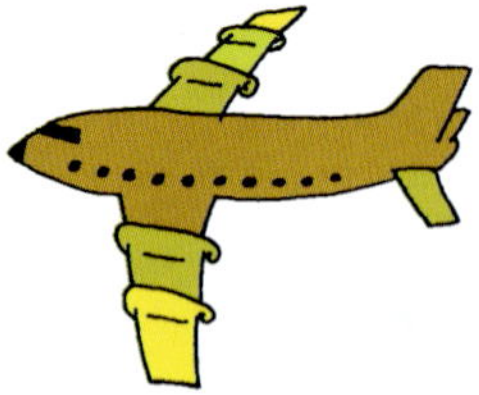 goes up.

plane

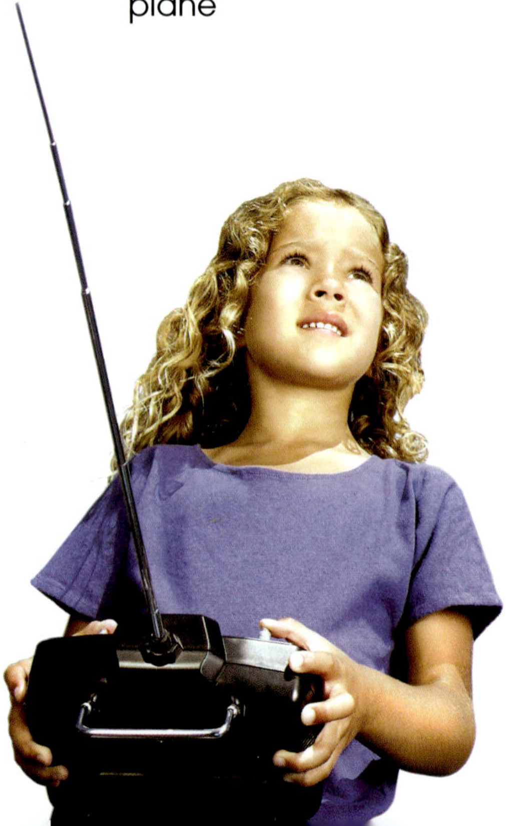

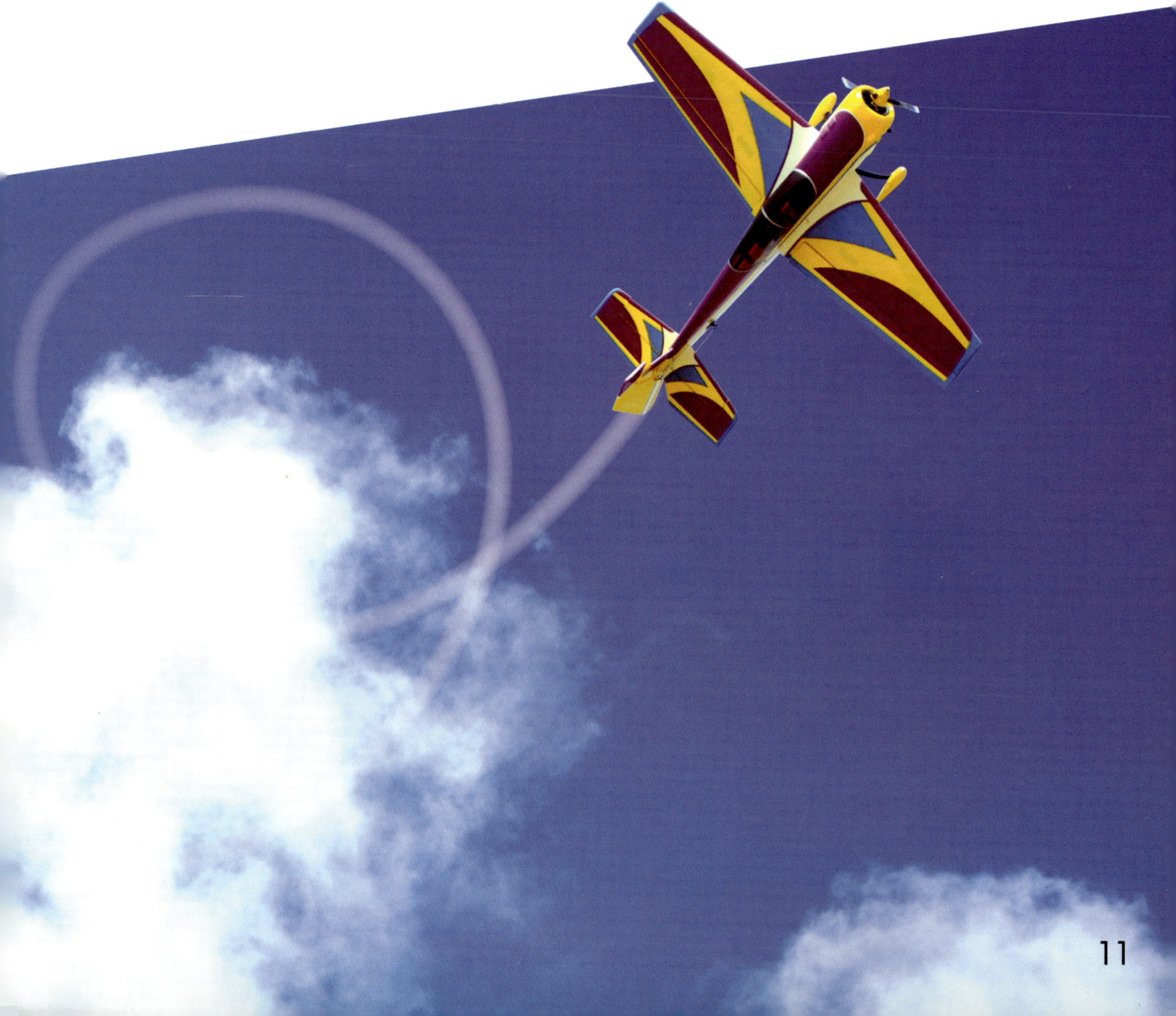

That 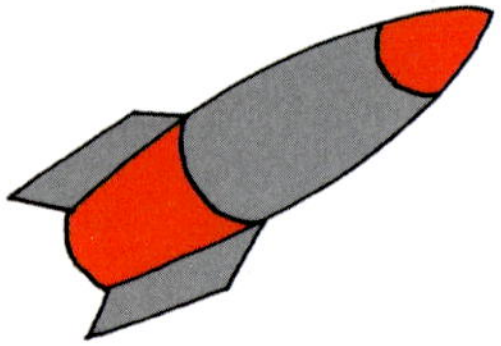 goes up.

rocket

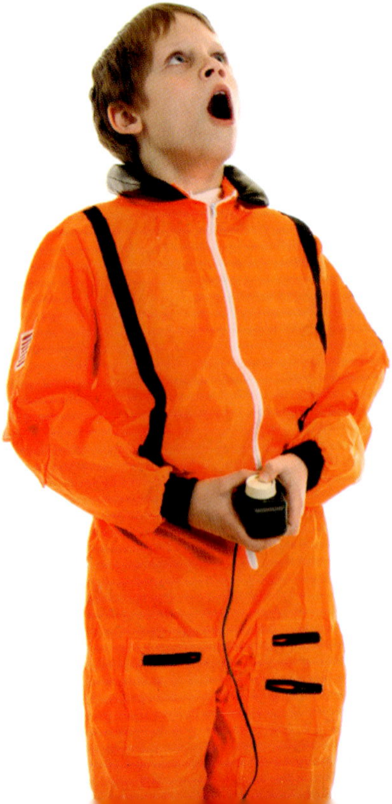

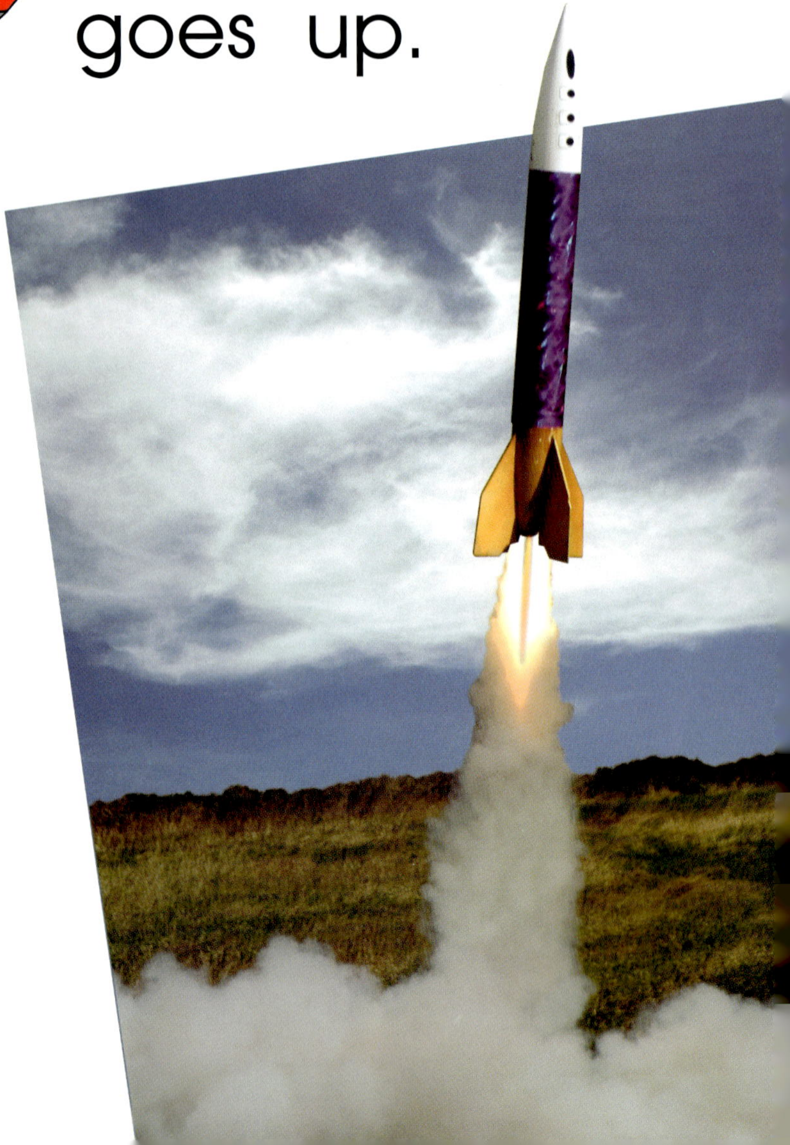